E $8.95
Kr   Kraft, Jim
              Garfield and the
           tiger

DATE DUE

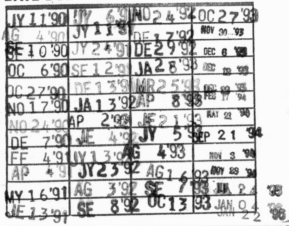

JY 11'90	JY 6'91	NO 24'92	OC 27'93
AG 4'90	JY 11'91	DE 1 7'92	NOV 30 '93
SE 10'90	JY 24'91	DE 29'92	DEC 6 '93
OC 6'90	SE 12'91	JA 28'93	DEC 13 '93
OC 27'90	DE 13'91	MR 25'93	DEC 22 '93
NO 17'90	JA 13'92	AP 8'93	FEB 17 '94
NO 24'90	AP 2'92	JE 21'93	MAY 22 '94
DE 7'90	JE 4'92	JY 5'93	SEP 21 '94
FE 4'91	JY 13'92	AG 4'93	NOV 3 '94
AP 4'91	JY 23'92	AG 16'93	NOV 28 '94
MY 16'91	AG 3'92	SE 7'93	JUL 24 '95
JE 13'91	SE 8'92	OC 13'93	JAN 04 '96 JAN 22 '96

GARFIELD
and the Tiger

GARFIELD
and the Tiger

Created by Jim Davis
Story by Jim Kraft

A Golden Book • New York
Western Publishing Company, Inc., Racine, Wisconsin 53404

"I love the circus,"
said Jon.
"There is so much
to see."

"I love it, too,"
said Garfield.
"There is so much
to eat."

"Look at the tigers,"
said Jon.
"They are very
handsome."
"Yes," said Garfield.
"They look like me!"

The tigers did tricks.
"Cats should not do tricks,"
said Garfield.
"Tricks are for dogs."

The show ended.
Garfield went to the tiger cages.
One tiger was named Bim.

"Why do you do tricks?"
asked Garfield.
"So they will feed me,"
said Bim.

"I do not do tricks,"
said Garfield.
"And I get all the food
I want."
"You are lucky," said Bim.
"Garfield," called Jon.
"It is time to go."

The next day
Jon was away.
Garfield was chasing Odie.
The doorbell rang.

There was Bim!
"I am tired of the circus,"
he said.
"I am tired of tricks.
I am moving in with you."

Bim moved in.
He did funny things.
He jumped on Jon's bed.
Garfield liked that.

Bim scared Odie.
Garfield liked that.

Bim rode a skateboard
in the house.
Garfield liked that.

Then Bim ate Garfield's food.
Garfield did not like that.

He sat in Garfield's chair.
Garfield did not like that.

He took Garfield's teddy bear!
Garfield did not like that
at all!
"That tiger must go!"
said Garfield.
He thought of a plan.

"Jon will be back today,"
said Garfield the next day.
"Jon will like you.
Jon likes circus tigers."

"Good," said Bim.
"He likes to see them
do tricks," said Garfield.
"Oh, no!" said Bim.
"I must go!"

Bim packed his bags.
"Where should I go?"
he said.
"Try the zoo,"
said Garfield.
"The zoo always needs tigers."
"Good-bye, Garfield," said Bim.
"Thanks for everything."

That week Garfield,
Odie, and Jon
went to the zoo.
Bim waved to them.

"I am happy!"
he said.
"I have lots of food.
And I do not do any tricks!"

"That tiger seems friendly,"
said Jon.
"Yes," said Garfield.
"He is friendly.
But you would not want
to live with him!"